NUDIE DUDIE

The Jiggy McCue books can be read in any order, but to get the most out of them (Jiggy and Co are a wee bit older in each one) we suggest you read them in the following order:

The Killer Underpants
The Toilet of Doom
The Meanest Genie
The Snottle
The Curse of the Poltergoose
Nudie Dudie
Neville the Devil
Ryan's Brain
The Iron, the Switch and the Broom Cupboard
Kid Swap
One for All and All for Lunch
Rudie Dudie (coming in 2010)

Visit Michael Lawrence's website:
www.wordybug.com

And find loads of Jiggy fun at:
www.jiggymccue.co.uk

A JIGGY McCUE STORY

NUDIE DUDIE

MICHAEL LAWRENCE

ORCHARD BOOKS

ORCHARD BOOKS
338 Euston Road, London NW1 3BH
Orchard Books Australia
Level 17/207 Kent Street, Sydney, NSW 2000

First published in 2004 by Orchard Books
This revised edition first published in 2009

ISBN 978 1 40830 406 8

1 2 3 4 5 6 7 8 9 10

Printed in Great Britain

Orchard Books is a division of Hachette Children's Books,
an Hachette UK company.

www.hachette.co.uk

For
all
teachers
librarians
parents
&
nudists
who
get
a
kick
out
of
the
Jiggy
books

CHAPTER ONE

Did you ever have a dream where there are people all around you and suddenly you're naked? I mean without a thing on. Totally starkers. Just you, no one else. Well count yourself lucky it was only a dream. Imagine if it happened in real life. Like it did to me.

It started the day Tony Baloney came to my school. Tony Baloney isn't his real name. I can't tell you his real name because he's quite famous. He's an actor in this TV soap about...

No, better not tell you that either, or you might guess who I'm talking about. Tony Baloney, under his real name, used to go to Ranting Lane School. He's the

only ex-Ranting Laner who ever made a name for himself, even though it's the name of someone who speaks words written by other people and moves the way other people tell him. Think about it. There you are, a fully-evolved humanicus beingus, with the ability to walk, speak, hum, scratch and cut your own toenails, and you get famous for doing as you're told. And for this job, for being a flesh-and-blood dummy, you get paid a fortune, get your picture in the papers, and get asked to visit your old school to tell the kids that money and fame aren't all they're cracked up to be, which means that on top of everything else you're a bad liar.

And guess what. Guess whose mother is such a big drooling fan that she tells her only son that if I ever want to eat or wear an ironed shirt again I have to get the prat's autograph in my father's *Help the Aged* autograph book.

So there I am, lunch break, the great Jiggy McCue, waiting with all these girls at the bottom of the steps from the main building, while Tone Balone stands at the top signing little books and scraps of paper. The Star has hair that looks like it came out of a box marked Bozo Hair, and a tan that has to have started life in a tin labelled Boot Polish, and teeth that obviously glow in the dark and startle moths. 'It's great to see you,' he says to every fan one after the other, and as they go he says: 'Keep watching the show!'

At the top of the steps, as close as she can get to Baloney without tearing his shirt off and chewing his chest hair (probably fake), is Miss Weeks, our Deputy Head. She's all shy and girly, fingers twitching like they'll fall off if

9

they don't touch him soon. I'm the only boy. The only male. And anyone who didn't know the real reason I'm there would think that I too am a fan of this git. It wouldn't have been so bad if Pete and Angie had been there. We could have made a big joke of all this. But they wouldn't come, even when I offered them money. So much for solidarity.

Miss Weeks saw me, and smiled, as if to say, 'So you're a fan too!' and I wanted to melt into the tarmac. But then someone came out of the building and said Miss W was wanted on the phone, and she excused herself and went in. Now it was just me and the adoring fans. I looked around for some sort of distraction, anything, not fussy, and saw someone standing next to me who hadn't been there a minute earlier.

This wasn't a Ranting Lane pupil. She

was a grown-up, and she had this short spiky hair and short spiky nose. She wore jeans that turned to rags just below the knee, and a T-shirt that screamed SAY NO, without saying what to. She stared up the steps at the Big Soap Star with this strange mixed expression, like she wanted to bury an adoring bread knife in his heart. She must have felt my eyes on her, because she glanced my way. The look in her eyes made me jump. They were so dark, yet bright too. If witches were real, I thought, this one would be chief cauldron-stirrer.

I cleared my throat. 'Fan?' I asked.

Instead of answering my friendly question she de-glanced and shoved through the girls to the top of the steps. Tony Baloney was surprised to find an adult suddenly at the head of the queue, but he said, 'Hi,' like he said to

everyone, 'I'm Tony Baloney, and you are…?'

'Your number two fan,' she tells him. 'Ophelia.'

For a sec there's panic in TB's eyes. But then he realises that Ophelia is her name, not a wish.

'Great to see you, Ophelia,' he says. 'Er…number two fan?'

'Seeing you in the flesh,' she replies, 'I know that you are your number one fan.'

Tony Baloney smiles, but it's a wobbly sort of smile. 'Do you have something for me to sign?'

'No,' she says. 'I brought you a present.'

'A present?'

She handed him a blue oblong box. 'You didn't acknowledge the other things I sent you,' she says. 'So when I heard you were coming to Ranting

Lane I thought I'd put this in your hands personally. That way I'd *know* you received it.'

There was something about the word 'know', the way she said it, that made the fans on the steps stop talking and a frown appear on Tony Baloney's brow.

'You've sent other things?'

'A black silk shirt, embroidered slippers, an electric fan,' Ophelia says.

'Electric fan?'

'It was a joke. A fan from a fan?'

'Oh yes. Ha-ha. Very good.'

'You don't remember getting it, do you?' Ophelia says. 'Or the other things.'

'Of course I do,' says Tony Baloney. 'But I receive an awful lot of things from fans…'

'Well now you have another thing,' she says, with a voice so icy you'd think we'd been swallowed up by a sudden iceberg.

13

T-Bal opens the blue oblong box. He blinks. Then he stares at what he sees, like he's having trouble believing his eyes.

'It's a pen,' Ophelia explains.

'Excellent,' Tony says. 'Thank you. I'll treasure it.'

'You're not supposed to treasure it,' the spiky fan snaps. 'You're supposed to write with it.' She sounds very angry.

'I will,' says Tone, giving her the sparkly old Baloney smile. 'As soon as my present pen runs out.'

'Oh, *sure* you will,' Ophelia says, spinning round and pushing her way down the steps. She walks quickly across the playground to the gates.

Just before Tony B closes the blue oblong box and drops it in his jacket pocket I think I hear him mutter, 'Cheap rubbish,' but I could be wrong about that. He turns the brilliant Baloney teeth on the next fan, a smaller one, who offers him the back of an envelope. Halfway through dashing off his moniker he stops. 'Damn. My pen's dried.' He frowns around. 'Anyone happen to have a…?' But then his frown clears. 'Oh, but I have a spare, don't I?'

And at the very moment he reaches into his pocket for the blue oblong box he's just been given, this stupendously stupid idea trampolines into my feeble excuse for a mind. *Lend him your pen. Mum'll love to think this wally used your pen to write his crummy name for her!*

I sprang into action. 'Use mine, use mine!'

Tony Baloney's hand freezes in his pocket and comes out empty. 'OK. Thanks.' He reaches down, over the heads of the fans, and takes my pen – just as the bell for the end of lunch break goes.

15

The fans on the steps started to get agitated right away. When the school bell goes it means GET TO CLASS AT ONCE, not GET TO CLASS AS SOON AS YOU'VE GOT SOME BIG-HEAD'S AUTOGRAPH. Tony Baloney wasn't bothered that the bell had gone. He carried on writing at his usual speed, one soapy signature after another, with my pen. As soon as he finished each one, the fan snatched it off him and ran to class. I would have gone too – not run though, running isn't cool – but he had my pen and I couldn't take it back after lending it to him.

The minutes clunked by. The playground had gone absolutely silent. Two more girlie fans to go, but these were bigger girls, who could probably stand up to the teachers. They took their time, chatting with Tony like they were thinking of kidnapping him and feeding him Turkish Delight till the ransom cheque arrived.

But at last they went and it was my turn. I was about to hand over the *Help the Aged* autograph book when the Big Baloney reached into his pocket and took out the blue oblong box.

'Here,' he said. 'Present for you.'

He seemed to have forgotten that I'd seen Spiky give it to him a short while before.

'No, it's OK,' I said. 'Really.'

'I insist,' he said, shoving the box in my hand like it was something he'd just fished out of the toilet. 'Now I must run.' He winked at me. 'I can't believe I came back to this dump voluntarily. Don't quote me!'

He didn't run, but he didn't hang about either. He was down the steps and across the playground in a flash, climbing into his sporty red car in the

teachers' car park. I stood at the top of the steps watching him go and wondering how, after all that, I'd failed to do what my mother had sent me there for.

Get the stiff's autograph.

I was about to enter the building with a weary sigh when the doors flew back and Miss Weeks leapt into my arms. She seemed quite startled about this. The farewell cuddle she'd been looking forward to hadn't been with me. She looked so disappointed to see the Star's exhaust fumes rising into the distance that you could have mistaken her face for an apple crumble.

But Miss Weeks was lucky. She might have missed a smooch with a smoothie, but she wasn't going to get a rollicking from her mother for not getting his autograph. In a minute she'd turn around and march back to normal life without any other big deals jumping into her path and spitting at her. Unlike me, she wasn't hours away from the most embarrassing pair of days of her life.

And I didn't even get my own pen back!

CHAPTER TWO

I did get one thing out of that autograph session, though. Detention. I'd kind of expected it when the bell went and I couldn't get to class. Last time I was late for one of his classes Face-Ache Dakin told me that if I was late for the next one it would be detention – and I was eight minutes late for the next one.

'But sir,' I said when he proved as good as his rotten word, 'I already have detention tonight with Mr Hurley.'

'Well now you have one on Monday as well, with me,' Face-Ache said. 'The way you're going, Master McCue, you'd better keep your diary free for some years to come.'

After school I went straight to Mr Hurley's room. Mr Hurley is our History teacher. He is not greatly loved. If there's one thing Mr H enjoys more than boring the sporrans off us with totally uninteresting things that have happened at some point in the past ten thousand years or so, it's dishing out detentions. Mine was for answering back. Answering back? I was just replying. You can't talk to that man.

I wasn't the only one in detention. My archest of enemies Bryan Ryan also filed in, along with Ian Pitwell, Terry Toklas and Martin Skinner. Skinner was a surprise. He's such a creepy-crawler that you can't imagine him ever getting in trouble. Turned out he'd asked to be there – yes, asked! – because he was writing an essay called *Being in Detention* and he needed to see what happened in it.

When Mr Hurley came in, Ryan said, 'You're late, sir. Detention!' Hurley asked him if he wanted to spend the entire evening there, and Ryan said he'd love to but his mum needed help with the sausage rolls.

'Sausage rolls?' said Hurley.

'It's my birthday on Sunday but she won't have time to get much ready tomorrow because she's working.'

'Don't forget to blow up the balloons, Bry-Ry,' I said.

Ryan threw his history book at me. I ducked. It hit Skinner. Skinner didn't seem to mind. 'Wow,' he said, 'so this is detention.'

'Enough!' Hurley bawled. 'You're not here to enjoy yourselves, you are here to be punished!'

'Thumb screws or Chinese Water Torture, sir?' I asked.

'Lines, McCue. One hundred. Two

hundred for the next boy who speaks.'

'I'm not saying a word,' said Toklas.

'Two hundred lines, Toklas,' said Hurley.

'Hey, that's not fair,' said Ryan.

'Two hundred, Ryan. Anyone else?'

I shook my head.

So did Pitwell.

So did Skinner.

'I'm starting a new system for detentions,' Mr H said, whipping some exercise books out of his briefcase. 'I want you to write your lines in these books, and when you've finished, and if I'm satisfied with them – if – I will keep them.'

'For old time's sake?' said Pitwell.

'As a record of who did what, when,' Hurley said.

'You didn't give Pitwell extra lines for cheeking, sir,' Ryan said.

'I'm not a harsh man,' smiled Hurley-

Burley with iron lips.

'Oh yeah, right,' muttered Ryan.

'Three hundred lines, Ryan.'

'This is fun,' said Skinner, writing it all down.

Hurley went round handing out the smart new exercise books. 'Your first task is to put all your names on the covers.'

'Can I ask a question without getting extra lines, sir?' I said.

'What is it, McCue?'

'Promise you won't give me extra lines.'

Mr Hurley stood over me, which must be quite a deal for him, because he's not very tall, and scowled down.

'I promise. Now what?'

'You said we have to write all our names on the covers. Do you mean I have to write Ryan's and Pitwell's and Toklas's as well as my own?'

'You're being facetious, McCue.'

'Yes, but I'm still on a hundred, you promised, I have witnesses.'

'Grrr,' said my favourite history teacher. Hurley hates being outwitted by us kids. He spun round and went to his desk, kicking a chair leg on the way.

'Sir, sir, I don't have a book, sir!' Skinner yelled.

'That's because you don't have any lines, lad,' Hurley said.

'I know, but if I'm sitting in on this and I have to write about what detention's like, I ought to do the lines as well.'

'You're volunteering to do a hundred lines?'

'You're a nutter,' said a small voice.

Hurley refocused. 'What did you call me, Toklas?'

'Not you. Skinner.'

Hurley was beginning to look a bit

frazzled. Well, he'd had a long hard day being stern with people. He turned back to Skinner.

'I'll have to go to the staff room and get a detention book for you then.'

'Thanks, sir,' Skinner said. 'Do the same for you sometime.'

Hurley went to the door, threatened to pull our toenails out five at a time if we moved or even squeaked, and vamoosed. We all looked at one another. Teacher gone, alone in room, big temptation to get up on desks and do a tap-dance, or maybe chalk something rude on the blackboard.

But Hurley was obviously in a mood to dish out lines till the cows left home, so instead we hung our jackets over the backs of our chairs and took out our pens. Well four of us did. The four included Skinner but not me. The reason it didn't include me was

27

that I'd lent mine to Tony Baloney to sign autographs with, and he'd pocketed it.

'Oh, brilliant,' I said.

'What is?' said Pitwell, who was nearest to me.

'No pen,' I said.

'H won't be pleased,' said Bry-Ry, instantly looking forward to the scene where I admitted to the History honcho that I was penless.

'Hang on, though.'

I'd remembered the pen T-Bal had given me in return for lending him mine for life. The spiky witch's gift pen. I took the oblong blue box out of my pocket and opened it. It was the first time I'd actually seen the pen. It had this dark-haired female type inside the transparent handle. I picked the pen up and tipped it, hoping it was what I thought it was. It was. When you turned the pen into the writing position the female type's clothes disappeared. I mean all of them. Totally. Every last bit of elastic. I laughed. For the first time in my life I was going to enjoy writing lines.

'What's so funny?' Pitwell asked.

I showed him. He laughed too.

'You can see everything!' he said. 'Turn her round.' I turned the pen round. 'Everything!'

Suddenly there were four of them leaning over my desk and ordering me to turn the pen this way and that.

'How much?' Ryan asked me.

'How much what?'

'How much you want for it?'

'Nothing,' I said.

His eyes popped. 'I can have it for nothing?'

'No, Ryan, you can't have it for nothing. You can't have it for anything.

It's not for sale. Specially to you.'

'How about me?' Pitwell asked.

'You couldn't afford it, Pitters.'

'Let's have a go, let's have a go, let's have a go!' said Toklas.

I slapped his hand. 'Get your thieving paws off. It's mine. I'm the only one who uses this pen, now or ever.'

The door opened. They scattered. Four rear ends slapped four chairs. Mr Hurley handed an exercise book to Skinner. He frowned when he noticed big grins on Skinner's face, Toklas's face, Ryan's face, and Pitwell's face.

'What are you lot grinning about?'

'So happy to be here, sir,' said Ryan.

'And you're not, McCue?' I was the only one who'd got my mouth under control. A real first.

'Detention's a serious business, sir,' I said, ultra-sincerely (I'd had lessons from a Soap Star).

'Glad one of you realises that,' Hurley said. 'Now get on with those lines.'

'Me too, sir?' said Skinner eagerly.

Mr H sighed. 'If you must, Skinner.'

He sat down at his desk and started going through homework books looking for things to find fault with, while the five of us got all set to write our lines in our exciting new detention books. The others were looking my way enviously, so I waggled the pen at them and made sure they saw the female type's clothes disappear before printing my name on the front cover. Then I opened the book to scrawl the first of my hundred lines. I knew what I had to write. Hurley had told me when he gave me the detention. *I must not answer back,* I wrote. *I must not answer back. I must not answer back.*

I'd written this a dozen times before the novelty of the stripper pen began to

wear off and I started wondering how many I should do before I could drop in the odd '*I must ~~not~~ answer back.*'

Suddenly I heard a gasp. It came from Skinner.

Then I heard other gasps, from Ryan, Tokkers and Pitwell.

I glanced up. They were staring at me with open mouths.

Mr Hurley must have heard the gasps too, because he also glanced up. When he saw where all eyes but mine were pointing he aimed his my way as well. And saw what the others saw.

'McCue...?'

'What?'

'When did you take your shirt off?'

'My shirt?'

I looked down. My shirt had disappeared. My bulging biceps and rippling pecs were exposed to the world.

But that wasn't all. Sitting at my

desk, looking down at myself, I could see something Mr H couldn't see from his desk. It wasn't just my shirt that had vanished. It was everything that answered to the name of clothe.

I was so shocked I jumped to my feet. My bare feet. My chair fell back with a clatter. Now Mr Hurley could see that it wasn't just my shirt that had taken a break. The others didn't seem to know whether to carry on gasping, point, yell, or what, so they did the lot, all at once, while Mr Hurley made a sort of death-rattle noise in his throat.

And me? What did I do? Well, my elbows jerked, my hips twitched, and my feet started to dance. This is what happens when I get agitated. That's why I'm called Jiggy if you're new here.

Everyone in the room was staring at my beauty spot. You know the one. First to get over the shock was Ryan. He

didn't understand where my clothes had gone, but Ryan has a small mind, probably because the only thing he uses his head for is smacking footballs.

'Anyone got an eggcup?' he chortled.

Hurley got his words back at last. 'McCue, what's going on? What's this all about? What are you playing at?'

Teachers seem to ask these questions of me quite a lot for some reason. I usually don't have answers. Like now. I looked about in panic. All I could think was that I had to cover the McCue twig and berries with something, anything.

Ah! My jacket, still hanging over the back of my chair. I snatched it up, put it on, pulled it across my chest. I felt a draft down below. The jacket was a couple of centimetres short. That's not an awful lot of centimetres, I know, but these were the couple I most needed. I took the jacket off again and wrapped its arms round my waist, with the buttons round the back.

'Ian,' I said to Pitwell, jigging in all directions at once. 'Button me up, will you?'

'Are you *insane*?' he said, folding his arms behind him.

Mr Hurley was burbling something, and I'm sure it was something fascinating, but I had other things on my mind just then. I jigged towards the door, backwards, holding my jacket closed over the McCue btm. There was even more yelling now, and some boyish laughter. The boyish laughter did not come from Mr H.

I was at the door and about to go out when I remembered the stripper pen. I couldn't leave it behind. If I left it behind, Ryan or one of the others would snaffle it and I'd never see it again. I rushed back to my desk,

dropped the pen in one of my jacket pockets, and threw myself at the door again. This time I didn't bother going backwards. Didn't seem much point really.

The corridor was empty, which was just as well. I jigged along it, dodging scattered drawing pins. I'd just reached the swing doors at the end when I felt something happening inside my jacket. I looked under the collar, which was hugging my belly button. My underpants had returned! It was hard not to choke with relief and gratitude. If nothing else came back, at least my party piece was back under cover.

But then...my trousers reappeared. And my shirt, and my tie (halfway towards my left ear where it belonged), and finally my socks and shoes. I was no longer nude, unless you count my head and hands.

My jigginess stopped.

I untied the arms of my jacket, put it on the right way, and walked out of school like nothing had happened. I was going to spend the entire weekend worrying about the big tub of hot water that would be waiting for me when I returned on Monday, but that was a detail. I was a whole lot more bothered by two or three other things. Like...

1. Why had my clothes disappeared?
2. Would they disappear again?
3. When?

CHAPTER THREE

Right after tea that evening, I left home. Well, for half an hour. As expected, my mother had thrown a wobbly about me not getting Tony Baloney's moniker. 'I don't ask much of you, Jiggy,' she wailed. 'Just one thing, one little thing, and can you do it? Ha! Shows how much you value *me*, doesn't it?'

Guilt went through me like a curly straw. 'I would have got it, Mum,' I whined. 'But the Star Part was off before I could ask him. He even took my pen, would you believe?'

She didn't want to hear. 'Just one tiny thing,' she said tragically. 'One itsy little thing. For your own mother.'

I was closing the gate when a little yellow car pulled up next door and Dawn Overton got out. Dawn's a student nurse at the District Hospital.

'Hi, Jiggy. How's tricks?'

I didn't know Dawn well, but she always said hello and I always said hello back because it would be rude not to. The truth was she brought me out in hot flushes. Mystery why. She was nineteen but looked more like fourteen, and she was quite small, like her car but not yellow. She had reddish hair and bluish eyes and a really nice mouth, but she was just a girl, so why would the blood spurt up my neck whenever she came within half a block of me?

I told her that tricks were great. It was a lie, but she didn't need to know that. 'Just finished work?' I asked as my cheeks burst into flame. Silly question, seeing as she was in her nursey-wursey togs.

She nodded. 'Long shift. Same again tomorrow. Sunday, though, I'm not getting up till at least eleven.'

'Eleven on a Sunday?' I said. 'That's the crack of dawn for me.' Then I thought, 'Dawn. Dawn. Why did I say *dawn*?' and scurried across the road with my head inside my shirt.

Over at Pete and Angie's we went to Angie's room, because it's a palace compared to Pete's, and smells better too. First time I'd spoken to them properly since morning break and they wanted to know all about Tony Baloney, even though they weren't fans. I didn't tell them much, but I did mention my mother's wobbly and the reason for it.

'You lent the prat your pen to write autographs with,' Angie said, 'and didn't get one for your mother, even though she asked you to *specially*?'

'Don't you start,' I said.

I also didn't tell them what happened in detention. I didn't understand what had happened myself, so explaining it would have got me nothing but grins and nudges from Pete and 'Oh yesses?' from Angie. When I'd told them all I was going to, the conversation sort of dried up. We tried to think of something to do till bed-time. The best anyone could come up with apart from watching TV was a game of Hangman. This was Angie's idea. Pete wasn't thrilled, but he spun towards the door and said, 'Come on then.'

'Come on where?' I said.

'My room. Where my computer is.'

'You don't need a computer to play Hangman,' Angie said.

'What other way is there?' said Pete.

'The original way. The paper and pencil way.'

Pete snorted. 'Paper and pencil! What

century are you *in*? I've got better things to do with my time.'

'Such as?'

'Things,' he said.

'Like?' she said.

'Things,' he said, and went to his room.

Angie found a piece of paper but she couldn't find a pencil. I asked if a pen would do. She supposed it would, and told me to think of a word. 'Asteroid,' I said, smart as a stoat.

'But don't tell me what it is.'

I thought of another word and counted the letters silently on my fingers. I took out my pen and drew ten dashes, one for each letter.

'What's that?' Angie asked.

'My word,' I said.

'I mean the pen.'

'It's a pen.'

'I never saw it before.'

43

'Present from Tony Baloney. A thank-you for lending him mine – which he kept, the swine.'

'Let's see.'

I turned the pen upright and handed it over. The female-type in the handle was fully clothed again by the time Angie took it, but there's no fooling her. She tilted the pen. The female-type's clothes disappeared.

'Pathetic,' she said.

'Yes,' I agreed, taking it back.

'B,' she said.

'What?' I said.

'My first letter. B.'

'Wrong,' I said, drawing the first bit of the gallows a stick figure would soon be hanging from if she didn't guess my word.

'T,' said Ange.

'I'll give you that,' I said generously, printing a capital 'T' on one of my dashes.

'H,' she said.

'Nope.' I drew another bit of gallows.

'Jig,' she said.

'That's not a letter,' I said.

'Jig,' she said again.

'What?' I said.

'Your clothes,' she said.

'What about them?' I said.

'You tell me,' she said.

I looked down at myself. I was sitting cross-legged on the floor without a stitch on.

'Eek!'

I changed the position of the piece of paper I'd been working on. I got up. Carefully. I backed away, holding the Hangman paper over the McCue fruit and veg. Angie's eyes followed me. Followed the paper.

'What happened to your togs?' she said.

'Search me,' I said.

'Angie,' said another voice.

The new voice belonged to the mouth that belonged to the face that belonged to the head that had just appeared round the edge of the door. Audrey Mint. Angie's mum.

'What?' Angie said.

'I wanted to ask about the…' Audrey trailed off. She'd noticed me standing by the bookcase with nothing on but a bit of paper. 'What's this?'

'We're playing Hangman,' Angie said.

'Hangman?'

'Strip Hangman. History homework.'

'History homework?'

'They used to play it in the eighteenth century. We were told to research it.'

'Oh,' Audrey said. 'Well,' she added, and removed her head from the gap in the door.

'Wonder what she wanted,' I said.

'You want me to call her back and ask?'

'No. I want you to chuck your dressing gown over.'

'It's too small for you.'

'Maybe so, but it'll make me very happy, and will you take your eyes off my hangman please?'

She didn't take her eyes off. They were glued to that piece of paper and refused to unstick. Even when she reached for her dressing gown she didn't take her peepers off. She came towards me, eyes burning twin holes in my clever disguise.

'Stop right there,' I said before she got too close. 'Just throw it.'

She threw the dressing gown. I reached for it. I missed. I edged sideways, paper still in place. I stooped. I picked up the dressing gown. As I did so I felt something moving under the piece of

paper. I looked down. 'Whew,' I said, dropping the dressing gown and the Hangman paper. I had underpants again.

Then my other clothes came back, piece by piece. Angie just stared while I became slowly decent again. Then her mouth opened. Questions were on the way. Questions I wouldn't have answers for. I walked quickly past her, out of the room, down the stairs, across the road. I needed to be alone.

Pete phoned later. I knew someone would, but I'd expected Angie more than anyone else. 'What's all this?' he asked.

'All what?'

'This nudie stuff.'

'What nudie stuff?'

'Ange said you stripped off during Hangman.'

'Oh, that. I was having a laugh with her.'

I'd been rehearsing this. I knew Pete better than he knew himself. Loves a joke, Pete, so long as it's not on him.

'A laugh?'

'Yeah. Girls! Fall for anything.'

There was a pause while he took this in. Then he chuckled. Then he said, 'Cool, nice one, ha-ha-ha,' and clicked off.

See? No prob. But Angie. Angie would be something else again. Whole different kettle of tadpoles, Ange. When the phone rang a couple of mins later I knew it was her because the ring sounded so angry. I considered not answering, but not for long. You don't ignore the Mint if you want to keep your bits facing the right way.

'WHAT'S THIS ABOUT HAVING A LAUGH AT MY EXPENSE!?' she bellowed in my lug.

'Ange…' I said.

'DON'T YOU ANGE ME!'

49

'I was laughing at *Pete*, Ange, not you.'

'YOU WERE LAUGHING AT...' She brought her voice down a notch or ten. 'Pete?'

'Yeah. He's so easy.'

'You weren't pulling my leg?'

'I wouldn't dare,' I said. 'Don't tell him, though, will you?'

'Our secret,' she said, and hung up.

Now you're probably wondering by now where I'd sent my brain for the weekend. You're thinking, 'This McCue is a head-case. He can't see what's in front of his eyes.' Well let me tell you, it's very easy to listen to someone's story and pick stuff out. But when you're the person the stuff is happening to it's not always so blindingly obvious. It certainly wasn't obvious to me. Fact was, I was too puzzled to think clearly. And worried. My clothes had disappeared twice without warning. That meant they could disappear again, and maybe again, also without warning.

And I hadn't a clue how to stop it happening.

CHAPTER FOUR

Next morning, Saturday morning, the first thing I did when I woke up was look under the duvet to see if I had anything on.

I hadn't!

But then I remembered that it had been so warm last night that I'd left my pyjamas in a heap on the floor. I let the duvet go and relaxed. As I lay there relaxing under the duvet the worries came back. If my clothes kept disappearing in public I might be anywhere when it happened. I might be on the bus, or shopping with my mother. I might be in school, a full classroom. I might be eating my sandwiches in the

playground. I might be in the Head's office being told off for being nude in detention. Imagine that! There's Mother Hubbard being all stern on his side of the desk and suddenly, on the other, I'm in the buff again.

But I was jumping ahead. I had the weekend to get through first. Two full days when the worst could happen and keep on happening. There was only one thing for it. I had to stay at home. No going out. No mixing with the general public. Not even any meetings with Pete and Angie.

'If Pete and Angie come round,' I said to my mother, 'don't let them in. Understand? Do not – I mean DO NOT – let them in. Tell them I'm ill. Tell them I'm busy. Tell them I've gone to see a dead relative or something. Tell them anything, but don't let them in.'

'I'll do nothing of the sort,' she said. Typical.

I'd gone downstairs in my dressing gown. Nervously. Stair by stair. Hands hovering in front of me to slap them over the privates if they suddenly became the publics. There was no telling when this naked thing would kick in. That's what I thought then anyway.

When I'd had breakfast I crawled back upstairs to get dressed. It looked like being a hot day, so I decided to chance the back garden. The best thing, I thought, would be to wear as little as possible so there'd be less to lose, but also as much as possible in case the disappearing clothes thing was only a one or two layer job. So I just put my shorts on (no shirt, no socks) and three pairs of pants.* With three pairs of underpants on, if only one or two layers disappeared I would still have my

---

* I put the shorts on *top* of my pants.

Incredible Hulk jocks on over my incredible hulk.

I went into the garden. Fortunately, my mother had cut the grass yesterday or she would have moaned at me until I did it. She was next door with Janet Overton (Dawn's mum) and their new dog, Charlie Farnsbarns. Dad was out front cleaning the car. You could hear him from two streets away, because he had some Golden Oldie rocker on the car radio. He wasn't cleaning the car because it's something he likes doing, or even because he thought it needed doing. He was cleaning it because my mother had ordered him to. He knows his place. But I bet he was grumbling as he worked. Grumbling something awful. Cleaning the family car is woman's work, Dad says. He hates doing stuff round the house too, like putting up shelves and things. The worst three letters in the English language for my father are DIY. He has another name for DIY stores. He calls them YDI shops.*

Anyway, with the grass already cut and Mum next door with Janet O, and Dad swabbing down the car out front, I had some time to myself. I took a deckchair and Dad's paper into the garden – and the pen Tony Baloney had given me. I was going to need a pen, because there's a no-brainer crossword in the *Daily Thing*, and Dad hadn't done it yet. The worst he could do when he found it already filled in was enrol me in the nearest orphanage, and I might not complain too much about that.

As I flopped into the deckchair a big seagull dropped out of the sky and landed on the fence. We're nowhere near the sea, but we get quite a lot of seagulls. They can't have a lot between

---

* You Do It.

the ears, if they have ears, or they'd realise you don't get all that many fish on housing estates, except indoors maybe, in glass bowls, or fridges.

'Lo, gull,' I said. It didn't reply. 'Suit yourself,' I muttered.

I did some crossword. I felt eyes on me. I looked up. The seagull was still on the fence, eyeballing me like it had never seen a perfect specimen of human boydom before. 'You're wasting your time,' I said. 'I don't have any fish for you. I don't even have any bread.'

I did some more crossword. I felt eyes on me. I looked up. The seagull was still fencing it. 'You want to watch where you park your tail, gullface,' I said. 'If Eejit or Jolyon see you it'll be Seagull Pie on the Atkins tea trays tonight.'*

After that I ignored my feathered friend and really got down to the crossword. Dad's record for the no-

---

* Eejit and Jolyon Atkins are our next-door neighbours, on the other side to Janet Overton.

brainer was twenty-six minutes, according to him. He was proud of that, even though it was called the Ten Minute Crossword. I'd already put in five minutes and in that time I'd only made sense of two clues, and I wasn't too sure about one of them. Either my father was brighter than he let on, or I was thicker than I thought. Every now and then, to help me think, I tipped the pen and watched the female-type's clothes come back. Then I tilted it the other way and watched them come off. While I tilted the pen and doodled in the margins of the paper, put in the odd letter, the sun beat my skin, and apart from the distant thud of Dad's radio, and the distant voices of Mum and Janet over the fence, and the odd stupid bark from Charlie Farnsbarns, the world was pretty peaceful. I could get used to this, I thought.

Some hopes.

I suddenly got cramp in my left foot. I shook it. The cramp stayed. I sighed. If I wanted to get rid of the cramp I'd have to haul myself out of the deckchair and walk round in circles for a while. I glanced at the fence. The seagull was still there. 'Bet you never get cramp when you sit in a deckchair doing your father's crossword,' I said. No answer, just the stare-out treatment, which to tell you the truth was starting to get to me. I hate being stared at.

I dropped the paper and pen on the grass and jerked out of the deckchair. I looked down at my left foot to tell it off for cramping me, but instead of telling it off I said: 'Hey.' I don't spend all that much time talking to my feet, but there was a reason this time. The reason was that the flip-flops that had been on my left foot and its best bud

Right Foot weren't there any more. I was barefoot. But that wasn't all. My flip-flops weren't the only things that had disappeared. My shorts and all three pairs of underpants were also just a memory. I was standing in the back garden of the McCue residence as naked as the day I was born, with the McCue parsnip and swedes waving in the breeze.

The only good thing about this was that I was alone. Or so I thought. I didn't count the seagull. But I should have, because the seagull had just noticed something to snack on. Something attached to me. Before I could gather my senses and jog into the house, the big bird gave a hungry squawk and swept towards me. Four more seconds and I'd have been barefooting the prickly doormat and diving into my mother's shiny plastic

apron with the picture of three blind mice on it. But four seconds was too long, because the gull had something I didn't. Two somethings. Well, three.

1. Wings. (Two)
2. A long pointy beak. (One)

The second of these (or the third, depending how you look at it) seemed pretty keen on snapping off my pride and joy and carrying it away without a by-your-leave. Would have too if I hadn't flipped round just in time, so that it hooked onto the McCue rump instead. I'm going to tell you something here. When a seagull sinks its beak into your bumbalina there's not a lot else you can think about for a while. But if you're like me you'll certainly have something to say. What I said went kind of like this:

AAAA!

The seagull squawked again, this time with shock, and debeaked. Then it flapped off to feather the nearest cloud while I scooted into the house clutching my wound. And as I got to the kitchen...

...my clothes reappeared.

This should have been a relief, but relief doesn't come easy when your sit-bit feels like it's been gripped by a spring-loaded clothes peg. It needed a good dose of cool.

I hauled the freezer door open and dropped the flap of the ice-making compartment. Then I ankled the shorts and triplicate underpants and introduced my tush to the box of SmartSave Multi-flavour Lollies. Ooh, the cold. Ooh, the blessed ice. I might have stood there forever if not for a sudden voice in the doorway.

'Jig,' the voice said. 'Why is your

bum in the freezer?'

'Warm day,' I replied.

'I prefer a cold beer myself.'

Dad opened the fridge next to the freezer and took a can out. He popped the ring pull, took a long gulp of beer, and left me.

But I wasn't alone for long.

'Jiggy, what was that screaming? What happened? What are you... doing?'

My mother. And Janet from next door. Gawping at my bare peach like they'd never seen one before.

'I was attacked,' I said, stooping in haste for my three pairs of pants and shorts. 'By a seagull.'

'A seagull?'

'In the garden. I was sunbathing.'

I covered myself. But not soon enough. My mother misses nothing.

'Jig, you're bleeding! The flesh is broken!'

'I'll live. Just.'

'Let me see.'

'You've seen all you're going to, get your hands off.'

'We must get you to hospital at once! You need a tetanus jab!'

'Tetanus jab?' I said, starting to jig. 'You mean as in…needle?'

'You can't be too careful,' Janet Overton said, like someone had asked her.

'No,' I said to Mum. 'No, no, no.'

'Yes,' she said to me. 'Yes, yes, yes.'

And that was it. It was decided. I was going to be done, like it or not, which I didn't.

Mum ran to the front door, bawled at Dad to stop what he was doing, and jogged upstairs. When she came down, brushing her hair, she threw a T-shirt at me. 'Put that on!'

'I can't put this on,' I said.

'Why not?' she said.

'It's one of yours.'

'What does it matter? It'll fit.'

'Mother, I am not going out with Josh Hartnett on my chest.'

She snarled, snatched the rag back, and hared upstairs for another. This time it was one of mine. A civilised one. Black. Lightning bolt on the front. I tugged it on. Then my mother drove me to A & E at two hundred miles an hour in a car covered in soap suds. I stood the whole time. Tricky in a car, specially when you're wearing a seat belt.

We passed the big sign for the hospital. Well actually, the sign said HOS ITAL. Someone had taken the P. There's always someone. By the time we parked the car and walked the six miles to Outpatients, my guard's van was throbbing so much that I felt like I'd grown an extra buttock. There were half a dozen other emergency cases

before me, so we had a bit of a wait. I stood up all the time looking at posters for warts. Kept half turning round to see if I'd caught fire. Sure felt like it.

During the wait I got more and more nervous about what was coming. When a lady nurse finally called me I thought that now would be a really terrific time to fall over and break my neck or arm or something so she'd have another part of me to look at instead. I didn't fall over, of course, but it was hard not to walk like my mother had found a new place to stash the rolling pin. The nurse led us to a little room with a curtain, like a changing room in a clothes shop but with a bed on wheels and fewer coat-hangers.

'Undress from the waist down and get up on the bed, please,' the nurse said.

'Do as you're told,' I said to my mother.

Mum smiled to make me feel better, and sat down on a chair. I asked her what she thought she was doing.

'Just sitting here,' she said.

'Up,' I said. 'Out,' I said. 'Scoot.'

She looked hurt. 'Don't you want me here?'

'Yes, I want you here instead of me, but if you don't want it to be you, please leave. Now.'

She went out. 'I'll be right here,' she said from the other side of the curtain.

'Triffic,' I said.

The nurse gave me a little cloth. I wiped my fevered brow with it.

'It's to cover yourself,' she said.

'You're kidding. I've seen bigger postage stamps.'

'When you're ready, lie face down. The doctor won't be long.'

She brushed the curtain aside and went out. I counted three, dropped my

shorts, then counted three again as I dropped my trio of pants. I got on the bed, on my front, and arranged the little cloth over my throbbing behind. I felt pretty stupid, I can tell you. From the other side of the curtain the nurse said:

'Are we ready for the doctor yet?'

'I don't know,' I said. 'Are we?'

She drew the curtain aside to let a thin man with a long chin and a white coat in. The nurse came too. My mother leaned sideways and waved at me. Nursey drew the curtain across. The doc smirked at me and peeled back the little cloth. He gazed at my mortal injury. So did the nurse.

'What's all this then?' the quack quacked.

'You don't know and you're a doctor?' I said.

'I mean what happened? Did you

sit on something?'

'I got beaked.'

'What?'

'You want the short version or the long?'

'The short would be nice.'

'OK. Seagull. Squawk. Snap. Here. You.'

'Well, we'd better give you a jab to be on the safe side.'

A jab. One of the shortest but most terrifying words in the human language.

'Couldn't you just give me a pill?' I asked.

He laughed. Well, he would, wouldn't he? He was on the blunt end of the needle. I couldn't look as the nurse unwrapped it and did whatever she had to do to get it ready to bang into my skin and out the other side. I rested my chin on my arms and stared at the wall. I needed

something to take my mind off this. There was a poster on the wall of an elephant's backside. Were they trying to tell me something? I heard a laugh on the other side of the curtain. My mother. And another laugh. Someone else. Nice to know everyone was so damn happy. Somewhere behind me and the elephant's backside a hand swabbed a bit of bare thigh, mine unfortunately, and the doc said, 'Just a little prick,' the way they do, and I said, 'You'll be hearing from my solicitor,' and then this spear was driving into me with the power of an Apollo rocket.

'There, that wasn't so bad, was it?' the doc said as he pulled the spear out a lifetime later.

'Not for you,' I gasped, turning sideways to thump my heart back to life.

'Nurse will wash and dress you now.'

'She'll do *what*?'

'The wound. Avoid beaks in future, that's my advice.'

'I'll try and remember that.'

Then I was alone with the nurse again. Ah well, I thought, I'll probably never see her again. But just before she got to work on my behind she said, 'I'm going to bring a student in, hope you don't mind,' and jerked the curtain aside before I could scream 'YES I DO MIND, I AM NOT THE CABARET!'

When the student nurse stepped in, my spine turned to fudge. It was Dawn Overton from next door. The very Dawn Overton who sent the blood orbiting round my ears when she said 'Hi,' 'Hello,' or 'Anything at all.' The Dawn Overton who winked at me over the nurse's shoulder before attaching her eyes to one of the two parts of my body

that I most like to keep under wraps when the neighbours are about.

Then the nurse said the worst thing in the world. She said, to Dawn:

'Think you can handle this?'

And it was Dawn Overton from next door who, very carefully, very slowly, placed the dressing on the McCue doughnut.

'OK?' she said to the nurse when the dressing was in place.

'Don't forget to tape it,' the nurse said.

'You want her to *video* it?' I said with horror.

Dawn laughed. So did the nurse. Oh, these HOS ITAL types are a jolly lot.

Then Dawn Overton from next door took a roll of tape and, even more slowly and carefully than before, like she wanted to make a day of it, or maybe a week, tore off bits of tape and stuck the dressing down. Every edge, every corner, with her own fingers, which had never even *touched* me before. Then she stood gazing at her work with a happy smile. At my back end.

Let me tell you, it was pretty hard not to die of total embarrassment just then.

CHAPTER FIVE

When we got home, Mum told me to go to bed and give the needle juice a chance to kick in. I went to my room to do as I was told, mainly because I wanted to hide myself away from human eyes until the end of eternity. The throbbing was wearing off by this time. I was beginning to feel like a two-buttock man again. This helped me think a bit more clearly, and thinking more clearly, it came to me at last (like it came to you ages ago) that all this started after I swapped pens with smarmy soap star Tony Baloney on the school steps. I went downstairs again, out to the garden. The pen was still

where I'd dropped it on the grass. Lucky Dad hadn't found it or I'd have had to break his fingers to get it off him.

I took the pen back up to my room and shut the door. I tilted the pen and watched the female type's clothes disappear. I looked down at myself. I still had my togs on.

So what made the thing work? Did you have to do something with it? Like use it? I reached for a comic and doodled in the corner. I looked down.

I hadn't a stitch on.

Almost, anyway. There was one bit of material that hadn't disappeared. The hospital dressing. I don't know why that stayed and nothing else did, but it didn't really matter. I understood everything else. If you tilted the pen and wrote or drew something you instantly became as nudified as the lady in the handle. The witch-fan who gave it to Tony Baloney must have hoped he'd sign autographs with it at school. She probably had it in for him for not answering her fan letters or writing to thank her for her gifts. She wanted to humiliate him, and nothing would have humiliated him more than standing at the top of his old school steps and suddenly having nothing on. He would probably have been arrested. If the newspapers got wind of it (and I bet the witch-fan planned to make sure they did) his career would have been ruined.

Even without an audience, I felt silly standing there in nothing but a hospital bandage. I put my dressing gown on and examined the pen. Closely. And noticed for the first time the lettering round the top, so tiny that I couldn't make out what it said without a magnifying glass. I dug out my magnifying glass (finest plastic) and peered through it, turning the pen

slowly round to read the two tiny words printed on it.

LITTLE DEVILS

That explained everything. Well, quite a lot. I thought I'd seen the last of Little Devils gear, but I was wrong.* I had to tell Pete and Angie. But not today. Suddenly I felt quite drained. The tet jab, I suppose. There was a rustling under my dressing gown. I opened up. 'Welcome back,' I said to my pants and shorts. They didn't answer.

I put the pen in its box and the box on top of the wardrobe out of harm's way. I sat down on my bed. Side-saddle. In a minute I stretched out, and that was the last I knew till Mum crept in and yanked the curtains closed. Once she was absolutely sure she'd woken me up she said, 'Sleep, Jig, it'll do you good,' and closed the door super-quietly behind her.

---

* To hear more about the Little Devils, you'll have to read *The Killer Underpants*. Sorry.

CHAPTER SIX

Angie phoned next morning.

'How is it?' she asked.

'How's what?'

'The keister.'

I groaned. Was nothing sacred? Had my mother stayed up all night printing posters to stick on trees and inform the entire world that her son's posterior had been gulled?

'I don't want to talk about it,' I said.

'Oh go on,' Angie said, showing her true colours.

'No.'

But I agreed to meet her and Pete, and got ready to go out. Mum said I ought to keep the dressing on and wear something

light so as not to aggravate the wound. I didn't need telling. Besides, there was no point putting on more than one pair of pants under my shorts when everything except the hospital dressing vanished when the stripper pen did its work.

Not that I planned to take any more chances with the pen. Now that I knew what it could do I knew what I had to do. I kept the box it came in because it was quite smart, but dropped the pen in the kitchen bin and watched it sink into a mess of cold spaghetti, and other nasties. If only all my problems could be solved this easily, I thought.

Fool!

I didn't feel too bad round the back today. Bit sore, but not too bad. I crossed the road to Pete and Angie's, walking more or less normally. It was Audrey who opened the door. When she saw me her face creased up with concern and her eyes tried to peer round me to look at my rear.

'How is it?' she asked.

I ground my teeth. 'It'll live. Angie and Pete about?'

'Go on up.'

'No, they can come down.' I didn't want her staring at my backside as I climbed the stairs.

Audrey yelled up.

'ANGIE! PETE! JIGGY'S HERE!'

Windows flew open all along the street, and a roadful of eyes locked onto my hind quarters. The population of the Brook Farm Estate did not yell with one concerned voice, 'HOW IS IT, JIGGYYYY?' but I bet they were tempted.

When P & A came down, I said I had stuff to tell them. 'Let's go to the park,' I said as we left the house.

'Why the park?' Pete asked.

83

'Because there aren't many people there.'

'You don't know that.'

'Usually there aren't.'

'Might be different today. Sunday. Warm.'

'Let's give it a whirl.'

I was in luck. The only people in the park when we got there were dots down by the boating lake. All the way I'd refused to say a word about what had happened since Tony Baloney gave me the pen, but once we got there I sat them on a bench and told them as much as they needed to know. I almost didn't get any further than Friday when I first lost my togs because Pete fell off the bench at the thought of a nude McCue in a Hurley detention. Angie didn't laugh, so I went on. One bit I missed out was the Dawn Overton and the Hospital Dressing scene. There's a limit to how much I'll share, even with my best friends, specially when it's stuff they'll still be chuckling over when we're queuing for our pensions at the last post office fifty-something years from now.

'A Little Devils pen, eh?' Angie said when I told her about the tiny lettering. 'Thought we'd heard the last of Little Devils.'

'Me too,' I said.

'And you dropped it in the bin?'

'Absolutely. Best place for it.'

'Never've known.'

'How do you mean?' I said.

'The clip of the one in your pocket looks just like the clip of the nudie pen.'

I looked down at my shirt pocket. I didn't remember putting a pen in there. But she was right. The clip did look like the nudie pen's. I took it out. It

was the nudie pen! And it was all slimy, like it'd recently seen the inside of a bin full of ex-food.

'Looks like you *imagined* you put it in the bin,' Pete said.

'Imagined it? Have you seen the state of it?'

'So you put it in and took it out again.'

'I didn't imagine it and I didn't take it out,' I said, wiping the pen on the grass. 'But think what you like.'

'If you binned it and didn't take it out again,' Angie said, 'it must have come back to you all by itself.'

'Must have,' I answered miserably.

'Unpredictable,' she said.

'What is?'

'Little Devils products. If we know nothing else about them we know that much.'

'Mm.'

I tilted the pen to see if the lady inside still lost her kit. She did. But there was one small difference. Previously she was looking away when her clothes skadoodled. This time... she winked at me. She did, I swear she did. I don't think Pete saw the wink, but he snatched the pen and turned it up and down and around with glee. He'd seen pens like this before, we all had, but that didn't stop him being keen to see one again. And again, and again, and again.

'Boys,' Angie sneered.

'Girls,' said Pete, leering at the pen.

'What I don't understand,' I said, 'is why it's come back to me. It didn't go back to Tony Baloney. I wish it had, then it'd be bothering him, not me.'

I vaguely noticed a middle-aged lady strolling along the path towards us with a poodle.* I also noticed another dog

---

* Might not have been a poodle. For all I know it was a Dwarf Great Dane with a really horrible haircut. I'm not good on dogs.

bounding towards them, some stray I suppose. When the stray reached them the woman scowled at it and it slunk off, head down, as if to say, 'I only wanted a bit of fun.'

'It's shaking,' Pete said.

'What is?' I said.

'The pen.'

We looked at the pen in his hand. Then we looked at the pen on the ground, because he'd just dropped it.

'Looks like it's getting ready to explode,' Angie said. Pete and I stepped smartly back. 'Pick it up, Jig.'

'It's going to explode and you want me to pick it up?' I said.

'I didn't say it was going to explode. I said it *looks* like it's going to explode.'

'So you pick it up.'

She did. 'Could be trying to tell us something,' she said as the pen continued to quiver in her hands.

'It's a pen,' Pete said. 'Pens don't have speakers. They don't have mouths. They don't talk.'

'It's a Little Devils pen,' Angie reminded him. 'Which means it probably has a will of its own and ways of communicating when it wants. Remember Jiggy's Little Devils underpants?'

Pete grinned. 'Oh, I remember Jiggy's Little Devils underpants.'

'Don't remind me,' I said.

Pete beamed moronically. 'Underpants,' he said. 'Underpants,' he said again. 'Underpants, underpants, underpants, underpowww!'

He said 'underpowww!' because I'd buried a fist in his shoulder – just as the middle-aged woman with the poodlish dog trotted by. I heard her say something as she passed. It might have been 'Hello, you three, lovely day for

89

a spot of high jinks in the park,' but it sounded more like 'Bloody hooligans' to me.

'Anyone got a piece of paper?' Angie asked.

'What for?' I said.

'Want to see if the pen will write anything.'

'Of course it'll write something. All you have to do is tip the stripper and words occur.'

'If it writes anything of its own, I mean.'

'Why would it do that?'

'It's a Little Devils pen. Who knows what it's capable of?'

No one had any paper, but there was some in a nearby wastebin and once Angie made me and Pete take a bit of it out and spread it on the ground, she got down on her knees to write. The pen stopped shaking as it wrote: *Sunday*.

July. Councillor Snit Memorial Park.

'The pen wrote that?' I said.

'No, I wrote that,' Angie said. 'I was hoping it would write something else in spite of what I tried to write, some sort of Devilish message. But it...didn't.'

As she said 'But it...didn't' the pen started to shake again. She put it down. It carried on shaking.

'Maybe it'll only communicate with its owner,' Pete said. 'You,' he added, to me, in case I'd forgotten.

Angie nodded. 'Give it a go, Jig.'

I picked up the pen. 'What shall I write?'

'Doesn't matter if the pen's going to take over and write something else,' Pete said.

'We don't know that it will, so I need something to write.'

'Try your name,' Angie said.

I leaned over the scrap of paper from

the bin. The pen stopped shaking. I wrote my name, then sat back and looked at it with the others. My name had become:

Didn't you know that it's rude to throw gifts away?

'We do now,' Angie said.

'We also know why it came back to me but not Baloney,' I said.

'We do?' said Pete.

'Yes. Because he didn't throw it away. He *gave* it away. Just like it was a gift to him from the fan, it was a gift to me from him.'

'And the only way you'll be able to get shot of it,' Angie said, 'is to make someone a present of it.'

'Right,' I said. 'Pete…'

I held out the pen. 'A little something for you.'

He jumped back. 'Get that thing away

from me!' But then he laughed. 'Some fashion statement.'

'Uh?'

He was looking at the front of my shorts, so naturally I did too.

'We forgot about that, didn't we?' said Angie, also looking.

There weren't any shorts. Not even any underpants. I was standing in the Councillor Snit Memorial Park in nothing but a bandage on my rear end.

'You disgusting boy!' yelled a voice from some way along.

The voice belonged to the woman with the poodley dog.

I dropped the pen and ran for the nearest tree, one hand over my front, the other over my bandage. I skidded round the back of the tree. It was occupied. The stray dog that had only wanted a bit of fun was cocking his leg there. He jumped when I appeared, and

when he jumped he spattered my leg.
Then he ran off, leaving me standing in
a pool of steaming dog widdle.

Barefoot.

CHAPTER SEVEN

Even though I was sure no one could see me, I felt kind of vulnerable behind that tree. Pete and Angie kept well away until my clothes returned, so people with binoculars wouldn't think they were with me. When I stepped out, fully dressed, with dogwet shoes, Angie pointed at my shirt pocket. 'Pen's back,' she said.

'Probably there for life unless I can offload it,' I said.

'Well until you do, don't use it,' said Pete. 'Not when we're around.'

'Spoilsport,' said Ange.

After the park we had nowhere to go, so we just drifted. In a while we passed

under the old railway bridge, which is known as…wait for it…The Old Railway Bridge. It's years since the last train went over the bridge, but families of pigeons live under it, high up in the girders. You know there's a lot of pigeons there because it looks like it's been snowing down below. And you only have to look up. My dad looked up once as he was walking under The Old Railway Bridge. He was on his way to see if he'd won anything in a raffle he'd bought a ticket for. When he looked up a pigeon sent him a message, right in the eye. Dad wasn't too happy about that, until he remembered that if a pigeon dumps on you it's supposed to be lucky. And guess what. He won the raffle. First prize. That's how come we have a stone gnome in our back garden.

I was a bit off our feathered friends just then, so I didn't hang about under the bridge, even for luck. On the other side of the bridge there's the old high street, or The Old High Street, which was the centre of town before the new shopping centre was built. Most of the shops there were pretty grim-looking these days, boarded up or vandalised, or both. One shop that was still open for business was the newsagent's. There was a sign on the door which read:

NO MORE THAN FOUR CHILDREN
AT A TIME ADMITTED
WITHOUT AN ADULT!

Pete decided it was chocolate time. He pushed the door back. 'Three!' he said loudly, and marched in. Ange and I followed, and just hung there in the shop while he chose his chocs. Up in one corner there was one of those round convex mirrors, which showed

everything in the shop, all distorted, including us. To make super-sure we'd be caught if we pocketed anything, the little camera high up on another wall watched us too. So did the old geezer and his old wife whose shop it was. Didn't take their beadies off us the whole time. They didn't smile or speak either, even to say 'Thanks' when Pete handed over the loot. I felt like a criminal just being there. Didn't this miserable pair realise that most of the thieves in the world are *adults*? There ought to be a different notice on their door:

**NO MORE THAN FOUR ADULTS
AT A TIME ADMITTED
WITHOUT A CHILD!**

Outside the shop we mooched until we came to the Honeybun Estate. The Honeybun Estate might have been a nice place once, when the houses were new and the street lamps worked, but times have moved on and different people live there now. Most of the gardens are overgrown, half the windows are smashed, and cars are dissolving into little heaps of rust on the kerbs. There's not a lot of movement on the Honeybun Estate. The reason why might be the satellite dishes. Satellite dishes breed faster than rabbits on Honeybun. That's a lot of TV channels to get through before you can get off the couch.

'Ryan's place,' Pete said suddenly.

'How do you know?' I asked.

'I came here once.'

'You came to Ryan's house? When? Why?'

'Coupla years ago. We were pals for four whole days.'

'First I've heard of it.'

'Me too,' said Ange.

99

'I don't tell you everything,' Pete said.

'Traitor,' I said.

'Firing squad?' Angie said to me.

'Guillotine first.'

'OK.'

'Then we cut his chocolate ration. For life.'

'Yes. Zap his chocolate ration. That'll teach him.'

'Wonder why there's a balloon on Ryan's knocker,' Pete said.

'It's his birthday,' I said. They glanced at me in surprise. 'He mentioned it in detention on Friday.'

'You should have told us,' Angie said. 'We could have gone out and looked at birthday cards we might have bought him if we liked him.'

We were about to turn back the way we'd come when the man himself appeared on the step.

'You three,' he bawled. 'This is

a private estate. No riff-raff.'

'You'd better move quick then,' Angie replied.

'Watch it, Minty,' said Ryan.

'Watch it yourself, Bry-Ry.'

'We came to wish you Unhappy Birthday,' Pete said.

'Bog off,' said Ryan.

We started to go. But then I remembered.

'Wait,' I whispered to Pete and Angie.

'What for?' they whispered back.

'The pen. I can't throw it away, but...'

Angie's face lit up. 'But you can *give* it away.'

'Riiiight,' said Pete.

We turned back. 'Bry-Ry,' I said. 'Got something for you.'

'Huh?'

'Present.'

As we kicked his rusty gate back and

strolled up his weedy path I took the pen out and waved it in the air.

'Your pen?' he said, recognising it even from a distance.

'You said you'd like it,' I said.

'You said you wouldn't sell it, specially to me.'

'Yeah, but it's your birthday. And I'm not selling it...' I stared hard at the Lady of the Pen. 'I'm GIVING it to you.'

And you know what? The Lady of the Pen looked right back at me, fully clothed, and smiled.

Ryan snatched the pen before I could change my mind. Tilted it. Watched the lady's clothes melt away. He looked pleased. But he was too suspicious to accept a gift from me just like that. We'd been enemies since the Infants. In all these years we'd never been nice to one another, ever.

'It's run out, hasn't it?' he said.

'It's out of ink.'

'No, it's not out of ink. Try it if you don't believe me.'

He reached behind him for something to write on. Grabbed a birthday card. Probably his only one.

We leaned over as he opened it. It was from his parents. One of them had written in it.

To our Bryan

Kissy-Wissies and Lovey-Doveys
from Mummy and Daddy
On Your Birthday   XXXXX

'Go on,' I said. 'Write something.'

Bry-Ry didn't write anything, he just scribbled. That's Ryan for you. But a scribble should do it, I thought.

'See?' I said, backing away with Pete and Angie. 'Plenty ink.'

We reached the gate. Safe distance. Ryan was still holding the birthday card in one hand, watching the Lady of the Pen do her stuff, no idea that things had changed quite a bit down below. Now he was perfectly dressed for the occasion.

In his birthday suit.

'Anyone got a thimble?' I said.

Ryan looked up, puzzled. He should have looked down instead. Under the card he was holding. His mum and dad looked down when they appeared in the doorway behind him. I don't know how Mummy reacted, but Daddy was still shouting as we reached the end of the street. Shouting at the birthday boy, not us. We laughed all the way home.

We'd just reached the estate when a little yellow car pulled up alongside. 'Hello, you three,' Dawn Overton said, leaning out.

'Finally dumped Big Ears then,

have you?' said Pete.

'Bet she never heard that before,' said Angie.

'How are you today?' Dawn said to me. 'How's the…?'

When she said 'How's the…?' her eyes settled on my shorts – and stayed there like there was a super powerful eye-magnet inside. She was seeing in glorious colour with surround-sound the bit of McCue that she'd taped on the hospital bed yesterday. All right, she'd only seen round the back, so it could have been worse, but when you're on the spot, on the kerb, being eyeballed by the girl next door who's seen more of you below the belt than anyone outside the boys' showers and your mother when you were little, it kind of makes you squirm. In my case, more than squirm. I didn't know where to put myself. How to stand. Which way to face.

105

'What's up?' Dawn asked as the blood rushed up my neck and bubbled in my ears. 'You've gone a funny colour.' She started to get out of the car. 'Is there anything I can do?'

I didn't answer. I couldn't. My tongue had swollen to the size of half a grapefruit. All I knew was that I had to get out of there. Get myself home. Hide myself away.

I bent my knees.

I kicked up my heels.

I lobbed my toes at the pavement.

I scooted off homeward without so much as a wave or a 'Be seeing you'.

In five minutes I was in bed with the duvet over my head. And that's where I planned to stay until the world forgot about me.

Or at least stopped asking about my rotten backside.

CHAPTER EIGHT

'He's pulling a fast one,' Dad said, looking down at me in bed next morning.

'Oh, and you'd know, wouldn't you?' Mum said.

'Yep,' he said proudly. 'When I was his age I pulled so many stunts like this that I thought of putting myself forward for the *Guinness Book of Records.*'

'Yes, well you're no expert on seagull bites.'

'Seagulls, no. But I was bitten by a tortoise once. Off school for days, I was.'

'A tortoise. Some fast one.'

'I'll have you know that tortoises

have very strong jaws.'

'But not beaks. Jiggy's staying in bed, and that's that.'

'What about the tet jab?'

'What about it?'

'Well wasn't it supposed to cure his backside?'

'I'm sure it helped. What he needs now is rest.'

My father shook his head at me. 'Got it made, haven't you, Jig?'

I just groaned and hoped I looked bloodless. I'd been up early, before they were, smoothing talcum powder into the pores of my face. It must have worked because Mum's own face suddenly turned into a ball of knitting, and she said, 'Oh, *look* at him,' and started stroking my pitiful brow like it was a stuffed cat.

Dad smirked. 'I've seen it all before. In the mirror.'

Mum stopped stroking and glared at him fiercely.

'Don't you have work to go to?'

'Don't you?' he said.

While they were glaring at one another I noticed that the palm of her hand, which was now lying face up on the duvet, had gone the colour of talcum powder. When I dropped my own hand into it to stop it getting itself noticed, Mum almost blubbed. I hadn't deliberately held her hand since my sixth birthday.

'Don't worry, darling,' she said. 'I'll stay and look after you.'

'But...school...' I said with my almost-dying breath.

'You can't go, Jiggy, and that's final. You're not leaving this house until I'm satisfied that you're better.'

Good old Mum. Falls for it every time.

I missed my Monday detention with

Face-Ache, but not much. Tuesday I was still over-acting like crazy and my mother was still believing every sigh and groan. I might try for stage school after Ranting Lane. Pete phoned late Tuesday afternoon to say that Ryan was in trouble.

'So what's new?' I said.

'With Mr Rice.'

'Woh.'

Mr Rice is Ryan's great hero, because Mr Rice is a big sporty type and Ryan thinks he is too. Bry-Ry likes to keep in with Rice, and most of the time he manages it. Sometimes, to see them together, you'd take them for father and son. Daddy Prat and Prat Junior.

'What did he do?' I asked Pete.

'Well, Rice was setting up a cricket match, and you know what Ryan says about cricket, girly sport, he says, and Ricipops said that seeing as cricket's not macho enough for him Bry-Ry could keep score. So he did, with…guess what?'

'Not…'

'Yes. The pen. And the first time someone made some runs and he wrote them down…'

A slow smile spread across my face.

I managed to get out of school Wednesday, Thursday and Friday too. Yes, five days in total. Five whole days. A school week. I could teach my father a thing or two about fast ones. By Friday night I was so rested, so well-fed, and I'd had my hair brushed so many times, that I felt like a different kid.

And then it was Saturday again, and I didn't have to act any more. I was all set for a miraculous recovery when…

No. I don't think I want to tell you about that. Nice neat happy ending for a change, why spoil it? I'll write it

down as a sort of record, but no one is to read it. I mean no one. And that includes you. You must look no further! Better still, just forget I said anything. Nothing happened afterwards, nothing at all, right? OK. Good. So long as we understand one another.

See you next time then.

Your friend...

Jiggy McCue

PRIVATE

TRESPASSING EYES
WILL BE PROSECUTED,
BY ORDER OF J. McCUE

Saturday morn. I'd phoned Pete and Angie under my pillow and arranged to meet them at ten. We were going to walk into town and hit the hot spots, like the ice cream parlour. Mum wouldn't have a problem with that. 'The air will do you good, darling,' she would say, stroking my cheek.

I was getting dressed when I heard the front door bell. I was completely dressed when Mum came up.

'Jiggy. Something for you. A get-well present.'

'A what?'

She came in. 'Friend of yours from school. He made me promise to put it in your hands personally and tell you it was a present. He said that twice. "Make sure you tell him it's a present", he said.'

'Who was it?'

'He didn't say. Said you'd know.'

'A present,' I said, taking it from her. 'Cool.'

It was very loosely wrapped. Took no effort at all to open it.

And there it was. In the palm of my hand. The pen, unboxed.

Mum leaned forward to take a squint. Because the Lady of the Pen was lying down, only half her clothes were missing. But half was enough. My mother's eager smile faded.

'I see,' she said, and in two seconds the door was closing behind her.

I was alone, and holding the Little Devils pen I'd given to Ryan. The same Little Devils pen which Ryan, the scumbag, had given back to me when he realised that he had to make someone a present of it if he wasn't going to become the official town nudist. And because the pen had returned to me as a present it was going to make my life a naked misery all over again.

Or was it? Hang on. It only did its stuff if you used it, if you wrote or drew or doodled with it. Well suppose I didn't use it. Suppose I...

'Uh?'

The pen had jumped into a semi-upright position in my hand and the rest of the stripper lady's clothes fell off. Then my hand was leading me across the room. Towards an open school exercise book. My hand reached out. The pen lowered. The nib was almost touching the paper. It was pretty obvious what was coming next.

'No!' I cried, trying to open my hand and shake the pen out.

But I couldn't!

It refused to be dropped!

The Little Devils nudie pen had evolved. Now it could make me pick it up and use it whenever it felt like it.

The nib touched the paper. Words started writing themselves. And as the words formed...

...my clothes disappeared.

I looked at the words on the paper. There were six.

Aren't you pleased to see me?

The stripper lady winked at me.

Look out for more JiGGY in 2010!

RuDiE DuDiE

A new drama teacher arrives at Ranting Lane School. Is Jiggy really going to have to play Bottom in the school production of *A Midsummer Night's Dream*?

And introducing a brand-new series...

...in which we meet a whole host of Jiggy's ancestors and discover that, through centuries past, there have *always* been Jiggy McCues!

Don't miss the first book,

where we meet a 13th century Jiggy...

Don't miss
the next exciting
JIGGY adventure...

NEViLLE
THE
DEViL

**TURN THE PAGE
TO READ THE BEGINNING...**

CHAPTER ONE

We were just pulling in to a motorway service station for a widdle-and-fodder break when I had this sudden feeling we were in for a bad time. There were seven of us in two cars, Mum and Dad and me in one, Pete and Angie and his dad (Oliver) and her mum (Audrey) in the other. The dads were driving. My mother says dads like to drive because the car is the only place they can feel in charge. When we pulled in, I rushed over to Pete and Angie and told them about my sudden feeling.

'You always have a feeling we're in for a bad time,' Angie said cheerfully.

'Not this sudden,' I said.

She pushed past me. 'Well this time you're wrong.'

'I wouldn't be so sure about that,' I said to her back.

She spun round, still cheerful. 'One more word,' she said, 'and I stick your head in the nearest litter bin. That'll be your bad time.'

'Relax, Jig,' said Pete, also cheerful. 'Nothing bad's going to happen. Not this time. I feel it in my armpits.'

I sighed. Maybe they were right. Maybe I was worrying about nothing. I dumped the nervous frown and switched back to Cheerful Mode. Berk. I should learn to trust my bad feelings. Specially the sudden ones.

I'd better tell you why we were so damn cheerful. We were going on our summer hols. Yep. And not just anywhere this time. This time we were going Abroad. I'd never been Abroad. Nor had Pete and Angie. Best of all, we were going by plane. We'd never been in a plane before either. We had this ten o'clock flight to catch, that's ten in the morning, and we had to check in at the airport two hours before takeoff, which had meant getting up with the birdies. Our big shiny plane would fly us over water and some land to JoyWorld. You've probably heard of JoyWorld. Amusement park the size of a small country, with hotels and lakes and all sorts of rides. We were going to stay in one of the hotels and walk round the lakes and go on things we hadn't even imagined yet. Some of the things we hadn't even imagined yet would swoop right up into the sky before crashing right down into the ground and give us the galloping hysterics just before we tottered off to throw up over a parent. We were really looking forward to that.

Like I said, there were seven of us, including the four Golden Oldies. I thought there should have been eight. Stallone had never been Abroad either, or in a plane. Stallone's our cat. But Mum said that if we took him out of the country he might have to go into quarantine when we brought him back and we wouldn't see him for ages. 'Let's take him with us,' said Dad, who's not a huge Stallone fan. We didn't of course. We left his bowl with Janet Overton next door. Stallone's, I mean, not Dad's. Stallone always goes where his bowl is. One of Stallone's favourite pastimes, bowling.

But I'm going to tell you something now, and I want you to pay attention. Are you listening? Right. Here it is. Do not, whatever you do, go on holiday with parents. Any parents. In fact, any adults. Ban them. Leave them at home handcuffed to freezers. Take them with you at your peril. You can let them pay for the tickets and all the rest, that's OK. You can let them organise everything, and give you a big fat wad of the folding stuff, or better still a credit card with your name on it, but never ever let them go with you. When they're not yelling at you, or smoothing your hair, or making plans for you to visit model villages, they're embarrassing you in public places. My mother is especially good at this.

'JIGGY!' she bawled at the motorway widdle-and-fodder joint, so loudly that every head for miles turned to stare at me coming out of the Gents. 'DID YOU WASH YOUR HANDS AFTER GOING TO THE TOILET?!'

It's parents that should be put in quarantine. Permanently.

It was as I was exiting the Gents and my mother was screeching that something unexpected happened. A big stripy beach ball bounced out of nowhere – bounce, bounce, bounce – and stopped dead at my feet so I had to jump over it. When I jumped I flung my arms out to save myself.

They closed around a two-metre-high plastic rabbit with a weight problem and tombstones for teeth. The Big Fat Bunny wobbled and started to fall forward. I held on, I don't know why. And over we went. It was a slow fall. You know, one of those slo-mo moves you see in action films. When my back finally smacked the ground, Big Fat Bunny was on top of me. He was heavy enough for me to feel kind of flat about things, but not so heavy that it stopped my ears working. I mention this because my ears heard this rattle-rattle-clink-clink sound all around. But then I noticed two Big Fat Bunny eyes staring into mine and stopped harking to rattle-rattle-clink-clink-type sounds. Up close those eyes were terrifying.

The BFB and I stopped staring into one another's eyes when security men hauled him off and jerked me to my feet. It was then that I realised what all the rattle-rattle-clink-clinking had been about. It had been about a million coins hitting the floor and rolling around looking for holes to drop though. These were the coins that had been put in the slot in Big Fat Bunny's plastic chest only to shoot out of a flap in its bunniferous bott when it flattened me. People were scrabbling like maniacs for the coins. Even Pete was on his knees filling his pockets until Angie grabbed his collar and lifted him into a twitching crouch.

And then my parents were there, and my mother was apologising humbly to the security men – apologising for me, her terrible son – and Dad was saying 'Well done, Jig,' with a smirk. When the Big Fat Bunny was upright again a few of the coin collectors came over guilty and formed an orderly queue to drop the coins back in his chest slot. I ducked under some arms and between some legs and scurried to the food counters to give people a chance to talk about me behind my back. Angie was just two steps behind.

'What happened there?' she asked at the first food counter.

'The Big Fat Bunny fell on me,' I said.

'You must have nudged it.'

'I didn't nudge it. I threw my arms round it.'

'What did you do that for? Love at first sight?'

'I was jumping over a ball. Grabbed the BFB to save myself.'

'What ball?'

'That ball.'

A young kid had caught up with the ball and was walking away with it held to his chest, a happy grin separating his cheeks. I wanted to shout, 'There's the culprit! Stare at him, not me!' But I didn't. I said: 'Great. Hash browns.'

I was struggling to pick up a hash brown with the big tweezers provided when Pete shunted up.

'It's not fair,' he said. 'Dad told me to put the money back.'

'I hope you did,' Angie said.

'I gave it to him to put back. Most of it.'

'You mean you kept some?'

Pete tapped his pocket. 'The odd bit and piece.'

'Peter Garrett,' she said, 'that is charity money.'

'I'm a charity, didn't I mention that?'

'Go and give the rest to your dad.'

'Why should I?'

She pasted her nose to his. 'Because I'm telling you to.'

Pete knows better than to argue with Angie Mint when she's nosing him. He shuffled off, grumbling.

It hadn't been easy, but I'd managed to tweezer three hash browns on to my plate by this time. Beans next. I dipped the giant spoon in the baked bean bucket.

'That must have been your sudden bad

feeling,' Angie said, examining wrappers for E-additives. 'That a charity bunny was gonna pulp you.'

'No, that wasn't it,' I said.

'It wasn't?'

'No. Don't think so.'

'You think the sudden bad feeling was for something that hasn't happened yet?' I nodded. 'What?'

I shrugged. 'Dunno.'

'Jiggy, we're heading for an airport.'

'I know.'

'And a plane.'

'I know.'

'Which will fly up into the air.'

'I know.'

'With us in it.'

'I know.'

'Maybe we should mention your bad feeling,' she said.

'I know. I mean who to?'

'The Golden Oldies, who else?'

'Tell our parents I had a sudden bad feeling as we're about to get on a plane?' I said. 'I don't think so.'

She grabbed a bundle of E-additives and we left it at that. Something was going to happen, something bad, but we couldn't tell a soul. We would just have to see if we survived. Or not.

CHAPTER TWO

Angie jumped cars for the second half of the journey. She did this because she was sick of sitting next to Pete. No one should be forced to sit with Pete for more than ten minutes. I know that better than anyone because I sit with him in class for hours every day. We're not supposed to talk in class, but you have to do something to take your mind off being there, which means I get quite a lot of earfuls of Garrett and his stupid jokes. I get into trouble all the time for just telling him to shut up. Teachers have no idea what it's like to be a kid. Specially a kid sitting next to Pete Garrett.

We were already running a bit late because Dad had hit a winning streak on the fruit machines at the service station. Oliver, Pete's dad, hadn't been in much of a hurry either, though he wasn't doing so well on the machine next door. We might not have left when we did if the mums hadn't nagged so much. That bit of lateness was bad enough, but three miles short of the airport we ran into slow-moving traffic.

'We'll never make it now,' Mum said, biting her nails.

'We'll make it,' said Dad. But he didn't sound too sure.

The traffic thinned out around the time the airport car park signs appeared. There were four car parks and we followed the sign for Car Park Three, which seemed a pretty good idea seeing as that was the one we were booked into. But at Car Park Three we found that our spaces, B87 and B88, had cars in them already. Parked cars. Dad and Oliver squealed to a halt beside a little blue hut where the man who ran the car park lived. They jumped out and stormed to the little blue window.

'Those spaces are booked for a week,' the man in the window said when they told him what was up.

'We know,' said Oliver. 'We booked them.'

The man asked what names the spaces had been booked in and checked his computer screen. 'Hanker and Wok,' he said.

'What?' said Dad and Oliver together.

'Wok. And Hanker. Not your names. Let's see your tickets.'

They marched to the cars for the tickets, which the women handed them. Then they marched back to the little hut. The man looked at the tickets.

'Wrong car park.'

'What?' said Dad and Ollie again. They were really getting the hang of that word.

'This is Car Park Four. You want Three. Go back to the last roundabout and this time follow the sign to Car Park Three.'

'We did follow the sign to Car Park Three,' Dad said. 'It pointed here.'

'Is that a fact?'

'Yes, it's a fact.'

'I have a thought,' the man said.

The dads leaned forward, keen to hear it.

'What I'm thinking,' the man said, 'is that when you get home after your holiday you go to an optician for two pairs of specs. Then you'll see the sign clearer next time.'

Dad and Oliver snarled, jumped back in the cars, and burnt rubber through the exit. And back at the roundabout? We all saw it, plain as day, the sign for Car Park Three pointing another way entirely.

'I swear…' said Dad.

'That won't help,' said Mum. 'We're cutting it really fine now.'

'I know.'

'Even with this mistake, even with the slow traffic, we wouldn't have been this pushed if some of us hadn't wasted so much time at that service station.'

'Yeah, Jig.' Dad glanced over his shoulder. 'You and the charity rabbit.'

'I don't mean him,' Mum said. 'I mean you and those rotten fruit machines.'

'I was winning!' Dad said, banging his foot down so hard our heads nearly came off.

Spaces B87 and B88 in the real Car Park Three were waiting for us, as empty and lonely as they should have been until we screeched into them. Everyone jumped out, bags were hauled, and we ran with them to the bus stop by the gate to catch the bus that was going to take us to the airport just in time to catch the plane. Except…

No bus.

'Now what?' said Oliver.

'Buses every five minutes,' said Audrey Mint, pointing to a notice which said that.

'You don't want to believe everything you read,' Dad said.

Oliver agreed. 'Remember the sign for Car Park Three.'

'We were wrong about that, that's all,' said Mum.

'Ha!' said Dad and Oll in perfect sync. They were like a double act today.

'We should be in our seats on the plane by now,' said Audrey.

'Relax,' said Oliver. 'They always allow extra time for late arrivals.'

When Dad backed him up on this, Mum and Audrey rolled their eyes. Pete and Angie and I said nothing. We've learnt over the years that when the Golden Oldies are stressed to make like wallpaper. That way we don't get picked on for absolutely nothing.

The little blue airport bus pulled in two minutes twenty-four seconds later. I timed it. The driver got down like he had all the time in the world and lobbed our bags into the belly of the bus. We got on in a hurry, like it would leave without us if we didn't, with or without the driver.

'You're leaving now, right?' Oliver said when the driver heaved himself slowly up into his seat.

'Couple minutes,' he said, opening *The Daily Buttock*.

'But our plane's about to take off!' said Audrey.

'Timetable,' said the driver.

'But we're the only passengers, what does it matter?' Dad said.

'Buses depart every five minutes. There's the notice.'

We sat rigid in our seats counting out the final two minutes.

'Time!' Oliver yelled on the dot.

The driver put his paper down, blew his nose, checked his eyebrows in the rear-view mirror, and drove slowly towards the exit.

'Can't you get a move on?' Dad said.

'Fifteen-mile-an-hour limit here,' the driver replied.

'Could've got there faster on a one-wheeled skateboard,' Pete whispered to us. Ange and I shook our heads at him. A warning to make like he didn't exist. If we'd known what was to come we might not have done that.

Now we come to the proof that my bad feelings should be paid attention to. I could go into a lot of detail about this, really spin it out, make a big thing of it, but that would bore you and it would bore me, so I'll give you the short version. By the time we got to the airport…

Our plane had gone!

'Bet you're feeling pretty pleased with yourself now,' Angie said to me when we'd got over the shock.

'Why would I be feeling pleased with myself?'

'Your sudden bad feeling.'

'I'd rather have caught the plane,' I said.

Pete didn't say a word about my sudden bad feeling or missing the plane. He just came and stood in front of me and screwed his face up like I'd made it happen, then kicked a suitcase. He got an earful for that from the next person in the queue, whose case it was.

'There must be other planes to JoyWorld,' said Audrey. 'It's a major holiday destination after all.'

'You can't just hop on another plane like it was the next bus,' Dad said.

'Well suppose Aud and I go and see,' Mum said.

'Yes, let's,' said Audrey. 'Better than standing round here.'

'Wasting your time,' said Oliver. 'The whole world wants to catch a plane at this time of year.'

They went anyway. They were gone quite a while. It was a while filled with faint hope. Mums are good at sorting stuff, we all knew that. We stood there, the five of us, waiting with the faint hope, tapping our feet to the Salvation Airforce band under the clock. Our spirits lifted when we saw the mothers shimmying back through the crowds queuing happily for planes that wouldn't leave without them.

Until we saw their faces.

'Not one empty seat for love or money,' said Mum.

'On a single airline,' said Audrey.

'Holiday time,' said Oliver. 'I told you.'

'Question is, what do we do now?' said Mum.

Read the rest of
Neville the Devil
to find out what happens next!

READ ALL THE HiLARiOUS
JiGGY McCUE BOOKS!

THE KiLLER UNDERPANTS	978 1 40830401 3
THE TOiLET OF DOOM	978 1 40830404 4
THE MEANEST GENiE	978 1 40830403 7
THE SNOTTLE	978 1 40830408 2
THE CURSE OF THE POLTERGOOSE	978 1 40830400 6
NUDiE DUDiE	978 1 40830406 8
NEViLLE THE DEViL	978 1 40830407 5
RYAN'S BRAiN	978 1 40830409 9
THE iRON, THE SWiTCH AND THE BROOM CUPBOARD	978 1 40830405 1
KiDSWAP	978 1 40830402 0
ONE FOR ALL AND ALL FOR LUNCH	978 1 84616956 4

All priced at £5.99